**CHANGING THE WORLD
ONE KITCHEN AT A TIME.**

**A SERIES PRESENTED
BY CHILDREN'S CULINARY INSTITUTE**

"Good food is the foundation of genuine happiness"
- G. Auguste Escoffier

What if you went to a restaurant and there was only one thing on the menu and the one thing you could order was whatever the chef felt like making that day?

"Cassoulet for everyone today"
If you say it right, it rhymes.

Cassoulet: a common French dish of white beans baked with meats; it takes its name from its cooking pot, the cassole d'Issel

You would not have a choice between fries
and apple slices, or between chicken and beef.
If the chefs menu says "escargot" then
that's what you will eat! Each day the chef might
have a different choice, but just one option a day.

Escargot : Edible land snail often
cooked with butter and garlic

What if the kitchen at your favorite restaurant was like a circus!
What if it was loud, dirty and unorganized? What if there was no way to know if your food was being prepared and cooked safely?

Nice, clean restaurants were not available to everyone during the early 1800s.

The cost of food was high and most people had to settle for what they called "corse food".

Kids are smart and know when something can be improved!

There is a good chance that this kind of restaurant wouldn't be your favorite anymore! You would probably want to make some changes to make it better.

Kitchens were like this in the 1800s. There would only be one choice of meal per day, and there was always soot from the fires. The soot made it hard to see and it irritated the eyes and lungs of the cooks. The chefs would usually be sweaty and grumpy.

The kitchens were dirty and there were always scraps of food around. Scraps of food would attract critters. It was common to see rats and other critters in these dirty kitchens.

"Turnspit Dogs" were dogs that were bred especially for the job of running in a wheel near the ceiling of the kitchen. This wheel would then turn the rotisserie of meat over the fire. Dogs on the ceiling, can you imagine?

In France in 1858, there was a young boy who loved art. He enjoyed spending his day painting. He went to work in his uncle's restaurant when he was only twelve years old!

He didn't know it yet, but he would change the whole world with his talents in culinary art and his desire that everyone be able to have wonderful food.

His name was G. Auguste Escoffier.

Claude Monet and Edgar Degas were also interested in painting at this time in France.

Auguste spent several years of his young life in his uncle's kitchen learning about food and restaurants. Kitchen work, or being a "chef", in the late 1800s was dirty work and it didn't pay very well.

Auguste worked hard and he found ways to blend his love of art with his growing love of food. He organized the kitchen workers and taught them better skills. One thing he taught the workers was how to drink healthy liquids so they wouldn't be so tired and worn down by the heat in the kitchens.

Transferable skills, also known as "portable skills," are qualities that can be transferred from one job to another.

When he was in his early 20's, Auguste was a soldier in the Franco-Prussian war. He was already a very good chef and so he got the job of "Chef de Cuisine" for the general staff. He was able to continue his growing skills and the high-ranking officers were pleased to be able to eat so well.

Franco- Prussian war

Jul 19, 1870 - May 10, 1871

Chef de Cuisine is also known as executive chef. Chef de Cuisine is in charge of all the functions in the kitchen. **Cuisine: a style or method of cooking.**

His experience as the Chef de Cuisine during the war gave him enough skills to be hired after the war as an Executive Chef. The Executive Chef is the one in charge of the whole kitchen and all the staff. This time he was hired at the famous "le Petit Moulin Rouge."

Working at this job gave him amazing opportunities to meet many people. The people who were very rich and in high society in Paris often requested that he cook for them at famous eating establishments all over the country.

Auguste created a dessert for a famous opera soprano named Nellie Melba. This dessert is still popular today. It is called "Peach Melba." Peach Melba: peaches and raspberry sauce over vanilla ice cream.

Auguste was busy cooking and managing kitchens for restaurants where kings and queens, famous singers and other performers ate. He was requested as head chef at some of the most elite restaurants, like "The Ritz". He was changing the way people dined. He wanted to make fine dining available to more people.

Auguste was able to organize the kitchen and workers so that everyone knew what they were supposed to do and everything was clean, especially the food. This made it easier for the restaurants to offer many food choices on the menu and even take requests from special guests.

The Emperor of Germany, Kaiser Wilhelm II said to Auguste, "I am the emperor of Germany but you are the emperor of chefs."

Auguste wrote a cook book and he taught many other cooks how to organize and clean their own kitchens. He created menus with many options so customers could have lots of choices.

More people started to think about being a chef and it became a respected career because of Auguste's influence. Nice dining became more accessible and more enjoyable.

Auguste's cook books were translated into many languages and have been used to teach and educate cooks all over the world.

Auguste was just a boy who loved art, but he was able to apply his talents and experience with art to cooking. He set an excellent standard for culinary artists to be able to follow. These standards are still seen in kitchens everywhere today. Wonderful food and elegant meals are now available to people everywhere.

Does cooking in the kitchen, and cooking for others bring you happiness?
Do you have an interest that you think you can learn more about and change things in the world for the better?

The five French mother sauces

Mother sauces serve as a base point for a variety of delicious dishes including veggies, fish, meat, casseroles, and pastas

Béchamel: Béchamel sauce is a sauce traditionally made from a white roux and milk. Béchamel may also be referred to as besciamella, besamel, or white sauce. French, Italian and Greek Béchamel sauce recipes include salt and nutmeg as a seasoning base.

Velouté: A velouté sauce is a savory sauce that is made from a roux and a light stock.

THE EMPEROR OF CHEFS

THE EMPEROR OF CHEFS

Espagnole: Espagnole is a classic brown sauce, typically made from brown stock, mirepoix, and tomatoes, and thickened with roux.

Hollandaise: Hollandaise sauce, formerly also called Dutch sauce, is an emulsion of egg yolk, melted butter, and lemon juice. It is usually seasoned with salt, and either white pepper or cayenne pepper.

Tomato: Tomato sauce can refer to many different sauces made primarily from tomatoes, usually to be served as part of a dish, rather than as a condiment.

About Children's Culinary Institute

Children's Culinary institute is a program that teaches avid home cooks how to reach out into their communities and teach children kitchen skills. We operate with our highest goal being the creation of a brighter food future for everyone . We build skills and reenforce the day to day school learning through hands on kitchen knowledge and confidence. Our secondary goal is to bring sustainability to families with time together, and greater health and sense of enrichment in communities. To become part of our community, and to teach with our curriculum, reach out to us and we will help take your skills and to reach out to others.

A Note from the Chef:
What Chef Auguste did for the culinary world, I will forever be grateful for what Chef Auguste did for the culinary world. He truly brought the art of fine dining, and the ability to express art, love, and happiness through food into a light it had never before seen. He started at the ground up, and left no part of the change untouched. He made life better for chefs, for the wealthy, and for the average. The way we dine today began with his hands. His efforts are truly appreciated by this chef, and I feel honored to be able to share his life's work with Jr. chefs everywhere so they can also recognize his contributions.
- Chef Arlena Strode

Made in the USA
Middletown, DE
26 March 2024

52069717R00018